TO MOVE BEYOND
WORDS IN THE **WIND**

TO BECOME
DREAMS IN THE **END**

DELMAR & **ICETON**

To Move Beyond Words in the Wind

Copyright © 2025 by DELMAR & ICETON.

MILTON & HUGO L.L.C.
4407 Park Ave., Suite 5
Union City, NJ 07087, USA

Website: *www. miltonandhugo.com*
Hotline: *1- 888-778-0033*
Email: *info@miltonandhugo.com*

Ordering Information:
Quantity sales. Special discounts are granted to corporations, associations, and other organizations. For more information on these discounts, please reach out to the publisher using the contact information provided above.

Library of Congress Control Number: 2025909216
ISBN-13:   979-8-89285-478-8   [Paperback Edition]
                 979-8-89285-477-1   [Digital Edition]

Rev. date: 04/14/2025

Years would pass before I'd return to an old use to be bustling mining town in southern West Virginia. We're id come to learn. Not all stories have an ending.

Was around the summer of 1996.

Being young yearning for the life of adventure. I would in time and beyond meet a very peculiar set of circumstances that would only make the answer more elusive to comprehend.

The day was like most with a cool morning breeze, and of haunting sounds of daily life in the distance. Being off the. Beaten path has its own surprises.

It was nestled down a gravel road with trees towering the branches and leaves acted as a sprawling canopy. During day like now very pleasant to look upon, but night. Adding a mounting suspense to an already mind provoking terror.

Standing at the roads edge with visions provoking the mind of impending doom.

Mustering up the courage as I remonted my bike I begin to pedal looking at all the vast darkness provide by what was once a welcoming thing, would only add to the mounting fear on this night.

As the moon rays would find their way through the thick canapy above ever so little it was to illuminate my way to see there was a bend beyond the. canopy's end.

My terror ever growing more intense as I begin to listen and pedal to a crawl. Taking a deep breath now becoming more attentive to sounds and compelled to come to a complete stop.

Listening, but only limbs and folage compelled to move by a suggestive wind is what I came to hear. As I remonted my bike to resume pedaling a few rotations of the chain, a different kind sound was heard resonating an eerie sinister that would shatter my focus.

With a chuckle I realized the shifting gravel beneath my bike was what caused me pure primal childlike terror.

Reframing from allowing my imagination to further take me down a rabbit hole, I summoned the courage to pedal on. Silencing the mounting terror with every push of the pedals, chain rotation, and my imagination running rapid and wild, as I need the canopy's end, realizing I was non intentionally slowing to a crawl.

Only to cause these sounds I had pleased to become silent, was now as if a full orchestra the sound of gravel begin to shift vividly and with such robust intent, not of my doing but by a force unseen by me. How long, why?, who, or what? At this moment was not a concern, to fleeing was was.

All I could do was brace for the impending doom as the sound of shifting approaching gravel producing an eerie tone. With out of fear or "this" had me I could not move. Seeming like eternity. As I would learn was a few minutes, coming aware to be greeted by a cars grill, head lights and a blearing horn deafening all sounds.

I got into the vehicle and proceeded to the house which insued a burage of inquiries of why I was just standing in middle of the road.

With and assigned response "I was thinking", beside bantering pursing even day lingering to nothing more then a thought.

The next morning looking down from the second story gazing upon the place where fear mentally manifested the earlier night. The banter from the night not concluding by dawns light compelled me to ask around.

I'd come to learn as most bussiness were in old buildings but long after the any recollection of any idea, some with promising provoking theories, leading to elusive answers... until...

As I noticed the day lingering fading into its grand sun set.

Something compelled me to venture down an old abandoned street by a single light in the distance, no time to waver I begin down the street. Coming upon a what appears to be a run down abandoned drugstore the lone light was what was left of a neon sign, just the something captured my attention in the dim flickering light inside.

As the door opened the rements of a time gone by, besides dust and outdated stock, it was a full operational drug store, my attention was drawn to a figure at the til.

After time of simple salutation, I asked why I came.. and EUREKA!!!!

The store clerk begin to set the tone...

There was a tale of a stranger that is said to roam the woods. After more indepth inquiring, to the best of the store clerks recollection. That what happened took place around the same area I had mine., before roads, and he vanished or many think parished in the woods. Being only a hospital newly to the area soon enough would attract big bussiness, Colebarins, workers, trains. All the things to grant life to a town. But he was on the cusp of such a transition.

The year was late 1800s, a man would come to town like so many and long after seeking out a life for them selves.

And so he did found land farmed and having a vast a.ount of land need hands to work, as he no longer could Alone so he seeked out help, bring him to a widow and a young child old enough to care for it self but far from how. That is how it would go for sometime the three would do the day to day . Grateful for the extra hand, but longing for the sounds of family and life.

Then like all tragedy illness would plague the county side, and first the mother would be become ill, as he would try to take on more chores, so did the child, soon there after the mother would succumb to the illness.

Life in the backwoods would return to normal for a time as winter raged on.

Then the child would be pleagued by this illness causing the man to think... as a day or two past realizing he'd have to leave to provide he choose to hastily pack for a what would be a small trek, on a warm day but not this day as snow covered all that could be seen. They ventured out. What took place is speculative, as before written journals were found depicting the events I have recounted.

As spring recked havoc with spring thaw, it was several weeks before any one could check on him by a neighbor. Find a hastily seen of ramsaking of things being packed, only turning to concern, for the mother and child.

Closet neighbors, came as many others went in search only being directed by a letter with a single lone word hospital impaled by a Bowie knife to the wall .The group split and some packed to track the path others two hospital.

By days end no living or dead, trace of them was found at the hospital, it was two or three days later word has been returned he had succumbed to what most had already decided early on... finding him where he couldn't go any further and laid, of course animals time decided they both parished. Only allowing elaborate robust theories as to what happened.

All different in context but same topic.

Seeing a feating glimpse of sunsets grand illumination, I made my way back to the same road that started me down a road of wonder that nothing is what it is and not every story has an ending.

Knowing I now don't have to fear what I now know enjoying the dimming fading light of the days end. I peddled with a confidence not to fear, not rushing, then as I came to the canopy's end I came to a stop not compelled but to bask in the nights beauty, I smirked and remonted my bike and rode with a gental pace. Only to be alerted by a stranger sound in the distance, causing me to come to a complete halt to listen. Just as simple as I stopped I begin to peddle like a bat out of hell hearing in the distance the cries of a child.

Years would pass before I'd return to an old use to be bustling mining town in southern West Virginia. Where I'd come to learn. Not all stories have an ending.

Was around 1996.

Being young yearning for the life of adventure. I would in time and beyond meet a very peculiar set of circumstances that would only make the answer more elusive to comprehend. As I woke to a brisk eerie chill persuading its way through century old cracks the aged hinges held enough, but years of rattling the shutters air off East River Mountain amazing they held together at all.

As the surroundings were being stripped by the winters brisk tantrums stripping away of their majestic cover allowing a passer by a small brief glimpse down CANOPY LANE..

Listening to the radio made a call for more of the same for the preceding days to fallow, as I got a coffee pondering how much longer would we endure this winters assault. I could see Movement out the corner of my eye. Breaking my thoughts of present matters to a figure moving through not in a rushed haste, more like a stroll along a calm place . I gazed wondering who, but having neighbors over the hill Northside of CANOPY INN. I begin to wonder why be out in this must have been a good reason, and except for a few longer thoughts of pondering wonder I proceed I ultimately decided didn't concern me.

As the morning went its mondaine way it normally had down CANOPY LANE. I strolled room to room checking the windows and shutters. Finding my self pondering the winter stranger would be as I found myself gazing out the east second story window perplexed to why as I turned to gaze above the stairs leading to the kitchen, I was halted by a picture of a mature lady but something so young was still visible. After a time I collected myself not certain but compelled to return to the window as the day past as night became present reality.

As the dark of night encroaching smothering the day revealing only the things the moons illuminate glow could touch would become visible, as I shook my head to unburden this mental burden. After rechecking the needed daily concerns. I found myself once again again pondering out side the same window just hours earlier a stranger had walked.

As I went to ascend the stairs I found myself more intently drawn to this portrait of the mature elegance of her young appearance. Only to proceed to the kitchen becoming even more lost in this portrait.

I do recall as a child aware of this portrait, but never with this intense need to see it, a Victorian lady bare chested and almost translucent vail covering her lower extremities. A very beautiful price. As i set to have coffee, a disturbance in the snow I could see by the illumination of the moon bending across the snow revealing streaks leading from the house.

As I gazed sightly being able through winters flurries make out where the trek was headed to a hill down toward the edge of CANOPY LANE meets the street. Perplexed as to who it could be as the night became dark as cold as the wind threw a brisk tantrum a person would avoid.. But curiosity got the better of me to compelling to venture out.

As I proceeded to keep my course and forge on as I left the lights of the house and not put long it was apparent that my only light would have been the moon, as I begin to get an calm eerie feeling as all time felt as if it stopped as a figure approached me, I was taken back, thinking back wasn't sure but looked as if someone fell over the hill I asked but the lady not by sight but voice told me she was the only one here.

So after I seen no further reason invited her to the house and she was welcome to wait back at the house.

That being agreed we made our way back to the INN down the LANE. After sometime we settled in I had coffee, she had coco. As we revealed in our lives, she said she was from the area and surprisingly just up the road. Leading me to want to ask why she was out but wasn't my concern. As time fulfilled it's purpose and begin to get late. I did offer lodging in a spare room, but I'm not sure what further as it was late.

I'd wake to find her in my arms a cover separating our bodies, trying to not wake her, I moved ever so slightly, but as she cleared her throat, knowing she is awake. I inquired the way we woke, for body heat to word off the chill (century old cracks) she did go to the room, but ultimately came back and spelt beside me.

As surveying the aftermath of fierce rage of winters flurry. Out the windows, and preparing a fire I hadn't gone out the day before as I should have so now Id have to, seeing I'd be just outside I left a note sayong I'll be back as she had just appeared to go back to sleep the sun was just making it's self known and the weather was tame for now.

As I reached the cole pile seeing the night left a cold thick ice shell covering it I begin to chip to crack ultimately shatter being capable of getting a few pieces til later after the sun releases winters firm grip...

As I was headed back treaking through my own icy snow covered tundra, the winds brisk tantrums whipping the snow that covered the hilltops in to a marvelous swirling dance. Surveying as I walked back, the West end corner of the INN begin to come in view. Delighted being so close having illusions of grandeur of stocking the smolding embers Cole's, teasing flames, enticing fire as the torrential wind wrecks havoc by whipping my jacket about.

As I begin to cover head almost the swirling tormental on sought of another's winters night. As I approached the basement door a sound of a door banging unlatched in the brisk winds caught my attention, as I watched it sway open then return to a smack and a few small thuds against the frame. As snow swirled I could see trekking steps leading away from the INN continuing down then back up and over the hill were pavement meets CANOPY LANE.

A the last second I saw a figure go over the hill figuring it was her, I did know where she lived, so figured I'd look when the weather broke. In the chill of he morn I realized she never did say nor did I ask why she was out in the snow that night?

Later in that night dawn came in bursting at the seams, making me feel better hearing the radio D.J. we are having a heat wave 9° to 15°. Leaving a smartass smirk and under my breath chuckle I proceeded to check the daily welfare of the century old INN. Viewing out side for winter remolding or landscaping. As I ascended the stairs while gazing out the window then onto the portrait as it greeted you eye to eye as you ascend the stairs bashfully with her eyes closed. My attention was soon distracted by a calm but brisk swift in session of knocks.

Upon coming to the door a man wary and tired greeted me with a warm harmless tone as salutations were exchanged we would make our way to the kitchen so as soon he could warm himself but what has him put in winters frozen grip as he took livations I had coffee and almost as soon as he sat down, he conveyed how he was looking for his daughter a younger woman with a kind heart and a simple beautiful mond how she had left and been a bit worried as everyone in the area knew her he just wanted to know she was ok.

I conveyed the young lady whom stayed the night as it was late, but the next morning she had left before knowing why she had ventured there. But I couldn't tell her simpleton way giving hope but not sure if it was her, after lingering a short time longer, he proposed best to keep looking and as I lead him put I pointed his in the direction she had went.

We parted ways taking a short time to watch him trek through the snow every step slowly fading in the swirling winter cheer, as I went to shut the door

I saw a walking staff, thinking he'll return as if that is her father then he also was up the road so I carried it in and just as I sat it against the wall, it was as if he turned to wave.and then turn his arms flung up in the air and like greeting an old friend they embraced. So I rushed to the door going to not wait and return his staff, As I opened the door nothing of them, I was very eager to go but again they live up the road.. ONLY causing swirls of pondering and nothing more then curiosity to slumber.

Only to be woken by a fallen shutter allowing dawns abundant piercing light to invasively illuminate my room. A freeze would take up residence in the area for a few weeks and besides recently taking interest in a portrait that has hung for as long as I can remember, besides day to day nothing would change.

But soon enough one morning the weather had lost its immense clutches of winters frozen torment, and I was able to pay attention to the old INN down the LANE with the same name. As life was beginning to reanimate, after a few days got everything looked after or aware of, the day way sunny and sweater weather but the suns illumination was all most desired.

As it had been sometime since both winter strangers had departed, I received the walking staff the father had left back to him and see.her again possibly as school was back in session.

So I made my way over the North East direction leading to the main road off CANOPY LANE.

After some time of course up and the down then up this road until I reached the top the road leveled out could tell it was an old county road seems it was a dead end houses one across from another some look lived in others certainly abandoned, as I walked I could hear a chain swaying and a dog bark, not knowing from where I begin to walk hastily toward the last house almost beyond my own effort.

It was a decapitated house, vegetation and growth appearing to be of some decades, as most were in disarray though a few still looked cared for, this one two porch was caved in and just as you can imagine a decapitated home would look. As I entered th gate to go around to the left side of the home I sat the walking staff down against the wall, as I ventured around thinking I hear laughter but nothing the breeze swaying trees, but no one, as I shook it off to get my bearings, a car approaches the house. I froze hoping they were lost it's a dead end. But it would come to a stop and someone got out. Thinking reach for the staff but that would expose me so I slid against the house and readied for...

A elderly woman by herself in awe of the walking staff I brought with me. Soon enough with my explanation why I'm there, how I got the stick, and kinda how it all begin. As I reveal her through the explanation her emotional tone was of broken joy and as I finished joyfully saddened. As she laid the walking staff against the house.

He didn't lie… was what she said before she smiled and begin what had happened.

All started about the early summer of 1947, the area was bustling with commerce, so jobs, family, home was almost a giving if that's what was in your future for some, but not her daughter. No matter how beautifully precious she was her heart was to kind, with a simpleton mind.

So any male show any interest she was love sick, everyone knew and sometimes irritating, it would amount to no more then filtration and never went to far, and we tried to give her a life as normal as we could. Some G.I.s came through there was one who by days end would have her needless to say like a love sick puppy as she was just a gullible loveable simpleton. And they would go out to Beckley then all parts else where.

She believed he'd return late summer came and went still she waited even a few guys tried to help her forget, but to no avail.

She wouldn't let the notion go. Fall would fallow again holiday celebration she went and had a grand times but longed for him, no letter no word, she still full of hope and certainty he loved her. Then it was first frost, now by this time it was of neighborhood chatter, wonder but most thinking they know... A letter arrived for her from some were far from southern West Virginia.

She was so smitten no one ever got to read it as she kept it private, talking often telling what he wrote but no one at the time read it. So that was a story until Christmas Eve night. She got ready left the house, and.thats where I lost her.

With a momentarily loss of composure, she collected herself. Seeming as it emotionally draining, but struggling on she continued.

Then my husband finding the note weather had worsen and not worried to much figured she was safe went to check and never would return. The solder returned two springs later a fine solder, a few accomodations and with a renewed hope explain that a fellow solder is the one that gave him the address, with a broken spirit wondered if he ever get back, and that he did had planned a great life, but joy was even shorter lived knowing what became of her. ONLY causing him to buy land and build a house in hopes of ever she would return home he's be down the road.

This causing me to wonder which house, and it use to be at the edge of CANOPY LANE, that is no longer there. As we inquired of anything further, she revealed a picture he's had painted of her and Everytime she recalled seeing it, the lady would age, smirking at me isn't that funny I thought, as we begin to part ways I asked of the letter, she took a deep breath and handed it to me with tears in her eyes, held the walking staff for a moment, and with a sigh she smiled said, "He didn't lie."

As she drove away I was compelled to read this letter.

As I scanned through it your normal, sentiments of a G.I.s missing love, then I get to the last paragraph, he ask her to meet him Christmas Day that hell be there. In an awestruck bewildered comprehension, was she the lady that I...

And being a taken back by her and the staff and her parting words, he didn't lie. As I was trying to make sense of all this and how I'm involved, the car returned.

Drawn my attention she was asking to know if the paining was there. Sightly puzzle I said I believe not describing it,. So we headed to the INN. As we arrived to the east window. And she was taken back by the view, until her eyes were eye to eye with the portrait, an like all composure was like st she broke down and tears . After momentary emotions she revealed that the G.I. had kept his word to paint her as she aged gracefully with him.. so he wouldn't be alone.

After the moment past and her composure had returned upon bidding fair well i asked about the walking stick, and she quickly asked where it was, I told her I don't remember grabbing it. With a deep sigh of almost relief told me that he said if the staff ever makes it home I found her.

As she drove away, I decide to retrieve that staff,that all changing as I encroach upon the front gate I was halted to a stop having a urge to leave it as he did keep his promise, as I reached into my back pocket I realized I still had the girls letter from the G.I., and only one Thing I could do delivery it now she's home. As I shut the light onto the mailbox teetering on a weathers stump.

As I returned home, I begin to reflect and again I found my self at the east stair case stopping to see the view out side the window only for my attention to be drawn to the portrait. Which now was a much younger woman and no translucent material to cover her lower extremities. And just as quick to realize what I seeing and the next blink was like it was always . I chuckled under my breath then reaching in my pocket I looked at the scrap peice of paper in my writing read I made it home but just like the painting it to would return to I'll be right back written on the page..

Not all stories happen down around the canopy, or originate with in its haunted walls, being around such places near and far many stories get passed down simply by child like banter, to scare to keep you at slumbers bay. Some just don't have a logical rhyme or reason, some just never fade always certainly relevant.

As present as today's coffee, thought to be child like banter, but hard press to say it is as many passerbys and hikers talked of seeing something..child like banter compelled me to remember the first few times I heard of such a fable tale,during my early ride around years.As I was road up the side of the mountain almost like some badge of horror or right to pass to hear this horrid tale.. winding back and forth up the mountain road crossing in to Virginia only then creat the mountain top back into West Virginia. As the car was shut off and only sly snickers and ragged breathing could be heard.

Taking use of the silence, suspense, terror a story would begin...

All life was easy going, certainly times were changing, but slow enough to enjoy the time it took to get there.

With change comes all sorts, jobs, buildings and certainly people. All building to suspense,a vivid mystery, and a well um. Conclusion..

So like all greats stories do child like joshing, to some terrifying realistic realization, Conjuring the mind for almost 40 years, to catch a glimpse of it.

The 1950s a man began to build a life after back on track after many failed attempts, investments, get rich schemes, he had tried and succeeded to fail, but always enough to get by for another certain failure. Eventually selling his interest in a few, semi lifelines and bought a farm land around Richland's, married had two children, life would continue to grow.

Was about a few years many farms fell belly up and sold little by little, yet he struggled through the financial collapse making every Sacrifice he could, to make ends meet.

One day a letter arrived and it appeared that the tide had changed, so as I was told a man wanted to lease his land and pay him to care for it. Simply the best options giving the economy.

Well there daughter had come home from school, surprised they weren't home, she went to the neighbors and stayed there til evening when the sun swirled the day into Neapolitan visions of night. She would stay the night, come the morning after the news revealed why.

Her parents not more then 5 miles wrecked car was torched and the debris was being cleared, from the road charged remains of mangled metal and charged remains.

Well certainly wouldn't be hard to understand a child of a loving family would now be orphaned. The man whom leased the property decided to honor his agreement and allowed her to stay in the only house she knew.

As most people all knew her. Small town, she would grow to be a once very driven to know, simply years preceding to want to go to the site of the wreck. So was a time people would take her, then time moved on and that became less possible and more a burden with unrealistic searches,at times becoming violent as if she never wanted to be a part as she would just walk up alone any hour, becoming something of a risk by the grief over the years carried on and it just got were it wasn't to safe as she was trying to stop cars motioning down this gully by holding here hands together. That was what she did each time she went there, soon enough to as they thought would end it. Went to look...

Nothing was found old bones of animals but no tightly griped hands as she would proclaim. Eventually she would be sent to a home, from the sale of the land, but even after would be said was seen wondering the rode, by passerbys and hikers.. with a little more mysterious noises ok screeching tires and meek cries for help. But that only added to speculation what really happened.

Well was a wreck of a fiery inferno and was discovered only one body remained in the car wreckage a door was open and the other two vanquished in the intense inferno that was the final report.

Well when she was away she never allowed the notion of no survivors, as if she knew a truth no one else was realizing. She was proclaiming and motioning holding hands tightly, and over time she drew this any time she could.with the center being two hands holding tightly.

Was thought maybe she did hear of the door was a open. As her days came to an end being found slump in a chair, would normally wonder the halls, eventually never speaking or motioning about it

Word returned about her passing was the evening gossip, and seems she hadn't been gone long before people were in debates of a little girl wondering the same direction, was it her, or a different little girl.? No one was certain when to see it, again stories over time.

Under the road is a cove and over the years weather or lose control over the road would go and so many did. Then a guardrail got put up. So now more a look out then grim haunting, as time and her memory would fade.

Then I heard it a few times the child of the cove, simply simple folk lore or child like superstition. She would appear many would swerve defensively, like being cut off guard. Yet all the stories remained the same.

A young lady in white would beckening your car to come to a stop, and upon you asking if she needs a ride her face would be revealed by her hair covering it and a old hideous hag would cause a person to eradecly drive into a ditch was the need for the guardrail, yet no one ever seriously injured.

Well would be time, story would be told many times many ways but same ending.. until one day a unforseen tire flat, no not by design simply worn treads. After calling for assistance, and waiting, as something was pulling him to the roads edge revealing the cove beneath the road, he and theother man decided to venture down being avid rock climbers, so they ventured over the edge. Propelling down to a sea of green on the meadows floor.

Upon preparing to ascend back up as the sun was setting and recalling stories heard of these parts. A walkie talkie fell past the dense brush and down in the cove. So he proceeded to propel further down to retrieve it.

Upon gathering his footing and saw a bright shine between the rocks removing a few to reveal what was so gleaming beneath them.. what he saw....

Caused him to radio a weird question request.....in a wary tone.

What was the girl always saying?...

The response in return was just as bizarre...

Two hands clinched tightly.

Another blistery gale force to sway a mighty oak, certainly not a chance of a dance with these tantrums from the artic north. Only to conclude with all its effort a racket of noise to sway century ol' lumber to the rhythm of rattling boards with the hum of that ol' song.

One to cause to get all warm and lost in some way to defy cabin fever. As I wondered around checking the windows, shutters, and shoveling the roof.. to avoid a collapse. I had made my way to the east end window, smirking as I glanced out then only to smirking glance at her portrait as I ascended the stairs to warn, wasnt til I tapped my coffee cup with the spoon, only to conjure a compelling recollection.

Seems a recent change since last time. As in what was then, is never was now in the literal way possible it's where the soda fountain was is now the never was shop. Sorta came up on it during a very odd day.

It all begin shortly after a story one night the kind you scare through distraction. was about a day like today blistery tenaciously unforgiving intent of winters torrid obsession toward world domination.

A man started his life as most any child in the dusty trails with horse oxen and covered wagon he learned to become of service doing most anything for a favor or a shilling. Doing what ever he could when any one needed a hand.

Even now being of the simple gullible disposition. since hearing of another claim striking a small fortune, would only seem right any other claim would produce something.

Now like most expeditions summing up to simple cons, being of a trust well a con could only go so far, and being possibly anxious may have propelled an end to a likely nefarious situation. As he was of the trust fund type of wealth. Alot of people preyed on this through the years, but again didn't get to far.

Now he's not always been so simple, na like I said before he was just like every kid, causing simple mischief, getting in a small dusting or two.

His parents were part of a shipping transport family company some say once surpassed Vanderbilt, then a simple deal.. well that's talk.

His life was starting to take shape with age of time he built a good reputation.

Well one night at a jamboree in the city square a quick word had a bullet response and two men down, by law was justified as in the aftermath the shooter was to simple to recall what and why it happened, so it was decided.

His lady friend whose honor he avenged, realized helping him learn basic language and recollection she had the aspirations to be a teacher. Would go that way for a few seasons as the flowers bloomed then weathered away so did the ways of youth.

One day he found his friend had left abruptly and being of a simple mind would stick to his routine she helped him remember, and he would carry on, waiting for alot of days to a few to figuring she had gotten busy. With his free leisure time from routine, the cons begin, like I said before they were simple, as most of the time knew of his reasons, and the family. So watch out for him.

Then a weird story begin to feather around about a claim opposite, of his mine was a small fortune in a golden vein extending the length from the cave's mouth to appetite.

Well would seem during a outing with a well traveled pirate fellow, to check his mine, this fellow came and revealed how shiny and certainly pure it was buy producing a small leather pouch with a few nuggets. As he told his epic ascend the pirate scaped a peice of the mysterious stone.

Seeing no silver shine and gold streaks, he also pre took in libations and common fire side stories. The next morning as they woke to the smell of coffee realizing their pirate fellow set sail before the tide went out as one sailor to another.

Reexamining the deal to find his side of the vain, it was decided when they got back and settled up then MR.SWIFTWATER, reminded him of the nefarious roose.

Knowing a truth they assisted in allowing him to get supplies at a discount. As they woke and set out the next morning to a illuminated scene of pansy's protruding through the snow in a vast expansion as the sun revealed a swirling sky of orange and red slowing revealing their silhouettes upon the vast white wasteland before them.

First night was non eventful, second night was a bit sleepless as his anxiety was causing him to suspect someone or something was tracking them. But, it would be this night he wish he had seized the warning of him. Fear of the dark.

After checking everything and settling down sometimes before the mom would pass the horizon, a commotion would cause a storm of concern as he looked and two guns being rapidly fired with a explorative to assure he was heard.

That would literally start the day and as far as MR.SWIFTWATER was concerned of the matter he had done more unspeakable nefarious outcomes. About a days excursion was all it took to find the location of the claim, upon the side of a mule trek trail to the opening.

Seeing the weather was being undecidedly despicable, but for that time seemed appeased.

Next morning after gear certainty they went in the cave entrance, was simply black as Cole, seriously was a Cole mine. His father acquired it as a payment and gave it to him knowing people always need Cole, he could have some type of living in case life was t fair when they departed him. But, that was still a few years off, no railroad yet...

After a few days, few very furious days of being covered in 100% Cole sut 0%gold dust.

MR. SWIFTWATER, realizing this was a dud in a last ditch effort to furiously begin to search, after some very animated expressions he produced pieces of gold colored stones convincing his mining partner that with more money he could get a crew of men and come back and take the golden nefarious from the grip of the mountain.

Some years went by when I first heard this story, chopping it up to a greedy con of bad luck. Until I walked down a street I was familiar with just not familiar with the Norman Rockwell painting I viewed before my eyes.

But I was compelled to what stood in the same place as the soda fountain/drug store that I remember resided there.

Surveying this window boarded up, caution tape around the porch post, a front door swaying back in forth with a busted ships porthole.with a smiley face proclaiming this was open. A loud crash caught my attention going to see if who ever was ok.

As I crossed the threshold, it was almost like everything was renovated, to look well appreciated, every shelf compartment once empty or now existent now has a purpose.

As I rounded the door way seeing a wonderours perplextion before me. A man greeted me a very scholar appearance. Listened to my story I just conveyed to you. After salutations and my reason for being present, and his reason for being where he once had not. Answering one and leading teasing another...

Certainly not all tales are as wonderoursly as they appear, Sometimes the truth is not always to be preplexngtonly believed.

This child's story begins as any before in the ever expanding new lands . Her father a successful sharecropper, always able to aquire a steady stream of income, not to say wasn't hard times til harvest. Getting by with his wife first whom was aspiring to be a teacher of some degree. So she helped get through the hard times teaching, only to share sometimes a simple loaf of bread for payment as times were hard for all drought being the catalyst...

So for a time this worked til the wife she was expecting, and was a rough time, limited ways to teach, or way to barter they found hard times. Then a daughter would arrive...

She was a joy of a child so quiet, yet aware of everything like a sponge, her father would forget something in a deal and on point she'd answer, seeing this she would be one part of the team as the mom could inquire around town, his daughter would as among her school chums, and now this was the norm for a while still young she was becoming something like Marjorie was to C.W Post.. one day run a co-op.

Town after town, telling the seasons of time passing by the crocus, not always certain by dogwoods, iris, buttercup, or pansy. These few would cause such an illusion to get caught in.

Her dad finally found a swell deal with MR.SWIFTWATER, a fellow in a bind and sold him some land, needed tending but eventually had a working farm still doing sharecropper, and just opened the co-op. Oh this be about her 7 year.

She meets the local boy who's family was in shipping and her dad took up right quickly, getting some business hauling during down time so on be expected she'd get fondly of him, he was a bit older but was a good kid always willing to give a hand in exchange for a favor or a shilling.

Well was about the time kids went off to explore, he being raised there was just a technical phrase, hell I say if not for her he'd have... Well who knows?...

Be when they were of younger times they'd disappear til the chow iron was ringing, leading to a cloud of dust from some direction they ventured or hiding in some hole in the wall.

Never did anything to bad, then few years later every so often they come back from one of many expeditions and find any number of foliage of colorful layers. Would go that way never leading as if any would knew for sure. Was like these two were ment for something becoming aware only to them.

Well as time would go forth proceeding with age and the simplicity of complications, becomes not logical. And we age...

Well certainly an adorations for him by her as she made were the once were inseparable, now wouldn't be, and from his part looked like a dotting friend. No matter what the event the weather she made sure she got to be around him, and in a way made a dance aways for her.

Well now she was coming into focus of the others, but no she did desire to attention of another but him, yet did amuse the gentleman callers. Was al about mid March most of the wild foliage was already or starting to return and slowly brush stroke by number colored vision before the horizon.

A jamboree was midway through, upon the young man and the daughter to get refreshments a cowhand from the West got a little belligerent in his un cordial remarks. Well trying to make a night rather then a fight he moved about with her, and at times confronted to try and deter the cowhand's already menising intent.

Almost, in diamonds and Cole.. with all that kind a pressure to aquire one it was felt here, as the made his way with her, standing off the front steps.

It came to pass, and not to many certain, who was quicker, or more accurate.? As for one shot made both lay out of this world, and only one would survive re-entry.

Well for every possibility she could, between school, chores,, she was there . She also revealed he fired in self defense and wasn't a killer, yet these words he knew nothing what they ment, as if his mind reverted to simpler logic, not to be detoured and the daughters helping with basics living education, at first was a joy helping him but eventually besides a few frequent(several months) visits this was what she would be contend with.

Well was some time as life had returned to some normalcy, town was getting opportunities from far of railroad noise. But the sounds were far enough in the distant future to not bother a worry over.

So she after assuring him she would return, her family and a few others more less gun hands started out. Not much would happen a few days into the excursion, other then some glaring of being watched, and a few trades, was as expected. Arriving in town before noon had to chime.

A fellow gun hand seem to have offered to escort the ladies, unknowing how obvious whom he was trying to get attention of. The party would see some of the same old dresses cloth of different designs and patterns, only to lead them in to a BAZAAR who's owner a MR. F.L.BAUM Who while the patrons gazed at the wonderours joys they have found, was partaking in a very delightful story of some child and her friends...

Was later the day an early dinner was had as a few decided get the wares back then only be one trip or try to rush early morning, it was decided some would go back, so the wife and daughter chosen to return this trip, mother so as to put away their wares. The daughter was wishing he was not how he was, thinking her self what to do, both would be fine choice as she knew well her simple friend, and now a another whom she can talk with, but even she could tell as time went on this choice would never get easy...

As she woke in a ditch as the sun swirled day into night, with minor scraps and a few aggressive bruises manged to get her composure after being woken by a horse, seeming to recognize her. After taken survey of what could be seen as day trembled into night. She collected what she could collect and chose a direction toward a horizon and set out.

Non eventful for a couple days, other then whom she was? Then lack of rations the horse would expire do to exhaustion, and she would go a day longer, as she begin to become unconscious and succumb to hunger with her last effort she tried to be seen as her eyes fell into uncertainty...

Being excitedly licked in reputation, startled her to wake, simotaniously reaching for... Realizing it was a dog, and upon holding him he laid gently on her lap. Calm until she let him free and he was gone.. taking survey of all around her. Seeing it's a camp but whose and why is she here? As the questions flourished through her mind, a suttle noise behind the bush made cause for concern, looking to hear left found a gun cocked it.

After a tense exchange the weapon was lowered leading to salutations and the mystery from the beginning, knowing who ever was she?

The time was spent explaining whom he was since realizing she had no story to tell herself.

So begins as a merchant through his growing up and by 14 never saw the green shores of Ireland again. By finding a wife and creating a grand family figured make my wealth and take them home. But all that riches is in someone else mine, everything I built I sold to chase a dream for my family. Becoming lost in his nostalgic topic, he broke topic suggestion of her need of a change of clothes.

She being aware not to allow an opportunity as the gun was still close, but the older chap never asked for it back allowing a slight chance to trust him. In her present state of uncertainty.

Through the next couple days learned they were waiting on a partner of his to return from a town trip. His wife has started with him but was overtaken by sickness, but many years after their daughter was born and the age to be of responsible help. As for his daughter he says she left one day to go scout and hunt a little and maybe she'll come back.

With a rustling coming across the ridge and down the mountain slope, the ol' merchant said that's this partner and they begin to start to load up. At first the partner wasn't seeing how she'd be of any help, but the ol' merchant insisted with his age to help him as his daughter would have tended to this. And it went like this awhile, she learned things about herself and was taught by the ol' merchant in archery, alchemy, geology, combat, marksmanship, and showmanship.

Well a few dogwood petals would come and go. Seems it wasn't going to take much longer before one choice would have to be made. On a well lit night all had settled down and after only her and the partner were awake and far enough that low tone voices wouldn't be heard.

After she begin to dose off, a great force grasp her body and with maximum effort wasn't enough to detour this primal desire.

In a haste of a moment she held her gun, and click after click.... Nothing...

He would proceed feeling her giving up slowly, until he heard her pace of her breathing start to slow, as he rose his dirty booze smelling breath from the nap of her neck looking in her eyes saw the reflection of the ol' merchant with a barrel unloading. Causing her to be covered in his brain matter.

After taking stock, he offered her a change of clothes he bought a time or two back. After returning she thanked him for the attire, and inquired was it more for his daughter.

That's when he tells her he believed the peice of... Well did something so she wouldn't come back. Reassuring her these clothes were bought with her in mind, revealing in an emotional tone that at times wondered if the two had met...

Well was about her year of 16, she had to go it alone the ol' merchant, knowing death was his asked to be left alone and only asked one request since she didn't have a name yet would she be ok being called Emily? She did leaving only far enough not to be noticed, but close enough to see when he was ready for the other place.

Having taught her a way she would do the circuit that wares traveled and.begin to cause her own legend on land certainly and sea also.

By doing so met a pirate simply by speaking of past explotes he was familiar with her story. In a odd way something was very familiar about him to her, but simply chopped it up to similarities.

Well a few years went by and she would have traveled sea to sea, close calls, notorious, and was a legend. By time she was back on the circuit, certainly would be tried, but seldom had to prove.

Was a short while she would come across this belligerent chap in a salon, challenged her to some shooting challenge and got two things certain that day. She could split a hair on a bees bum, and don't blink. Of course he was drunk sobering the next morning in the jail arm bandage, and told she wasn't in a good mood and didn't act til acted upon.

By this time she was gone, the pirate along for the ride. Each making their ways along. Til one rainy night begins and not look to slowing by 2nd night wind crept in a dusty gale force kind. Relaxed the two had prepared and waited the weather out, a rustling of a horse and rider approached one to greet as the other hid guns drawn soon would turn into a night of fire talk still worried of an ambush yet no reason where they are on the plato. As the night went on the rider whom we come to know as MR. SWIFTWATER a man of a lot of stories all exciting and more exciting then the ones they conveyed. Then it was one…

About a gullible fool, who had gold in a mine and wasn't aware. Being so vague wasn't what made it interesting, it was the place and something about this person. But short thought and proceeded a few days as the ground was quick mud, horses wheels, and boots, almost became Lost.

She begin to inquire directions as he was enjoying some affordable friendly charitable libations.

As dawn approached she decided to go find this person, maybe get rich.

The two travelers traveled in that direction once her pirate friend saw it wasn't. Anything she couldn't handle, parted ways said he be back.

By a day later she arrived on the outskirts of town, being distracted by a failed chipped painted windmill for the well. Stopping to fill her canteen, as time seemed a bit still away.

After a few stops came into town after stabbling her horse not sure how long she'd be here, begin looking for this man MR. SWIFTWATER spoke about. After an hour or so and not seeing a familiar face,she went in the bar, and a weird...request for coffee.

Well after acquired, after a huge fee... she looked in the mirror and say a familiar face and with out thinking went to him, approaching him, before she could speak, he very cordial welcome her to dinner. Seeming her search was over. After a few inquiries about MR. SWIFTWATER it certainly was.

He inquired if she was sent to help him she concur, seeing how trusting he was all she could do as if something changed within her, as now isn't about riches but something...

They would partake in fire side chat and make plans, as from time to time a few stopped by to check on him but now also to see who this rugged wild woman was, as he had no one as he never needed one he had a whole town...

After simple correspondence, most took to her well some hoping she'd stick around.

After further inquiries into this mysterious gold vein. It was truth but supposably was killed coming back, odd thing his horse and gear was miles away from where he was found... But it was true gold was found... Leading to the possibility... compelling him to gather his tools,supplies. The weather has been far so in the hasted rush. They left as soon as the butter cups, and iris bloom.

The time spent together in her begin to cause her act gitty and almost in a smitten manner, realizing she would find her thoughts lost in a glance of him.

Was the first night after checking all was fine they sat down for some fireside thoughts, and begin to get lost as night went on she became the way no man ever made her tease her feminine desires as she embraced him as it was a slight chill on this moonless night using that coy deception to get close. Yet when she had hoped for wasn't to be found, as like a child he was so innocent. She broke down and he held her rocking her reassuring her he'd get the bad man who hurt her.. continue holding through the night. She would wake with the sun already high in the sky, and being offered coffee and that was it no questions to anything the night before.

Would seem to threaten, weather but besides a breeze and small temperature drop of the mountain height, weather was simply marvelous.

Later that night a flash storm came in, and not aware some stuff would be washed away, in a quick haste got most, and as they set to take stock a satchel was seen washing down the hill side. He instantly went to grab it. But missing it completely took off after it down the hill.

Was a time away but gathered as much herself and made her way to the mountains edge, hoping he'd come this way upon his return seeing she was gone.

The flash rain has stopped opening the sky to a vast blackness of insignificant sparkling.

As the rain began to stop running off foliage, a heavy step was heard veraciously making way through the darken scenery around, she grab her gun waiting and just as he became visible her gun fell causing the barrels to point to the ground as she laid them.

Going to him and seeing he needed to get out of the clothes, to avoid frostbite, or hyperthermia. Being below the cave she made sure he was ok and comfortable as she went back retrieving the supplies. After multiple returns finally got everything secured. Her being cold and him being warm for some time she stripped and laid with him, as he was in and out of consciousness.

Was the 3 rd day she woke to the smell of coffee and a cordial voice and simple joshing...

But taking a concern in him see he was ok for now. Leading to her getting clothed. A low breath chuckle from the pirate ended with a intensive stare from her.

After seeing maybe able to leave in days not weeks. The questions begin, how did the pirate know of the gold, only to reference became to check him out as he's been doing it since that day... in awe struck about this day of its importance. That day MR. SWIFTWATER, spoke about a treasure was aware of the other side on private family estate. But wasn't referring to him, explaining he never considered him simple actually more normal then most…

As the day lingered on he begin to get better as it seemed, during the vigil and looking for libations to ward off the cold. She came across a book like journal, begin reading a few pages.

And before long asked in a almost certain tone.. was this person related the one in the book.

An with a light chuckle informed yes... explaining she use to live here leading to knowing the true story of why she woke with the ol' merchant, up to were he saw here and looked after her. And the reason he is as he is.

As her face dropped into her hands in dispare, the pirate gave her a hug, she reciprocated in a tight embrace. After the sentimental truth. She finished reading the book, seeming reassuring what was already told. She decided to go back get him medicine as now he needs a doctor, the pirate agreed to wait 3 days then will have to go, aware full pack horse 2 days, light packed horse day… She left that night the land looking almost chameleon like every direction.

By the next morning found a familiar path even though it had been years since last seen, as the next night begin to come into focus. With limited supplies to carry her horse would be left from exhaustion, and carry on by foot as what seemed eternity, a glimmer of hope was coming in focus as she was taking a small rest, only to slowly see things get blurry and fade to black.

She a woken in a very warm room, with a young boy eager to know if she was a fearless warrior. After a few answering of questions from him, a woman came to tend shoeing him away. After a short time she be the in to ask where she was, to her limited joy was in town. But soon distraught by the realization of how long she has been there 2 days, in a semi frantic need to get ready and leave after hearing this left that journal handing it to the boy.

As no one was prepared and giving the town knew him usually he was alright… so no one choose to help but did in rations as he is known to under pack…

As she left in a blind haste what should have taken a few hours and see the mountain ridge, but not this time dence cloud cover made visual reference travel points obsolete, as she rode with a fierce devotion that she was certain death was coming for him giving the time away, slowly tracking on, the snow made trekking hard to maneuver, some by horse some by leading, until she came upon a painted fence post she knew of but not well to know where. Begin raging into the darkness, after a few times in the distance begin to hear a clicking of a pick axe hitting rock and fallowed it only unaware going deeper away,wasn't till she saw dogwood trees with a few simple initials, now up to this point she couldn't recall, but what mattered she knew well now... As for a moment the world went quiet, enough to hear a faint clanking of a pick hitting rock, only coming from a distance behind her leaving a l her mule as he couldn't continue doing to exhaustion. She moved between taps as she got closer it got fainter...

As I was talking with the scholar gentleman behind the counter. As he, assured me that was the, ending my story needed.

Only to make me question all these, stories. And it all started by some kids telling stories to scare. And the murders well summed up to, drunken ignorance All these crimes.... If you wanna believe that.

Be wary with a cautionary predictional care of a teddy bear. As we become enamored in a very eerie tale, hold your silly grizzley close. As autumn breeze begin to loose it's warm for the activity of the warm only to implicate a burdening submissive dominant for some, for others .football. Across the places near and far.

As all hollow eve nears so do stories of ghost, and terror in the night, for some every for few most often.

But can't be denied we all have been scared by our own imagination and the imagination of others.

Well here is a tale to maybe cause a tingle or two to let you know your still among the living...

As the town was beginning to remove the jamboree some few nights ago. The town was sleepy not much happens, simply only sports, a few times other scholastic achievement will be recognized, but only long enough to know the score, kinda get the picture. That is how this town operates it's clock by seasons of sports and those minor achievements seem to fill that small gap between seasonal play.. If they don't make playoffs, well it's plays, recitals, and jamborees.

Well that is all good and well as this year they got a kid with the arm of a... Well I don't know exactly but the kid can throw.

Well last year was a hard ending won state for his middle 8 grade... now he's up here, but some thing very peculiar about him says he sees all that well spirits and such, good thing I guess there is a lot that sometimes happens but we most accept it no were no outer worldly we just have a way to think some just aren't ready to pass on to the other place...

As a brisk swirl of season moved across the already yellowing along the street. The peice of the jamboree were being dismantle and taken away revealing the only green patch of grass year round, well kinda was started by these two boys.. hooking one of those computraptions up to the public video info system and we watched a good game and then a movie, but by <u>4AM</u> well the school bus driver was late as he watched his movie on that there panavox wide screen. So needless to say it became sport center...

Watching all our guys go from me high a grass hopper, to something that can only be said as a miracle, so they say... Um personally I think it's all part of luck draw of the stars, why just the other day I'll have you know I was reading...

As your attention was drawn to a couple friends out thrown the ball red shirt one done and some numbers on a white shirt, executing plays as if you were watching a simulation. The quarter back simply on point cause him self all kinds of mental turmoil as he shimmed and and darted and as he made a fact and using the momental of the action to propell the pigskin high disappearing in the dense clouds then. Almost like intended fell almost like it was designed.

Astonished I had to see more.. as I was trying to catch.up with him...

So there you are ill have you know I was reading about how those there killers on those were born on special days and if others we gonna be just a like em.. see my uncle Henry once said he and a killer guy I don't remember his name..

As a noise got him off subject.. see here my momma she tell ya.. whom be that killer fellow uncle Henry and that killer fella, she laughed and simply said he sat next to an actor who acted as a real killer. They just had coffee in some Utah town with a tummy b tones...

Well you gonna keep wasting? She asked not directly implying to anyone, as she handed me a grocery bag, then him and we were headed down past the court house square.

Looking around to seewere they had gone. But to no avail I lost them. Along the way as the wind gust to a slight breeze back and forth as I learned more and more about what was so special about this town.. besides football…

So why are you here, after 35 minutes already being back at his family home actually a very well kept home. His mother inquired.

Well I am a collector of sorts, whit a giggle response. That was well for a time.. the season was a great one the boys got to play seems the same type of stuff the boys did that day well seems they were watching and they both are laying now.. as I try to get away from my very informative town greeter.

I see him out in a field just at it so seeing a chance I went to understand why this kid was so special. As I slow encroaching not to break his concentration, he forced my hand to give him mine as a ball last second cought…

Good catch so why fallow me..? Most would left but you stayed why? In a very curious intent as the wind begin to whip he said give me 40 yards, I tried fell short about 10 yards but did get it in the net… Well at least your a straight shooter. As he gathered his equipment said well wanna eat.. as he walked back across to the nice well kept residence a modest farm home.

We partook in dinner, and he aloud me to see more about his success in sports, and he asked why I was there? This time seems he was aware, just then his perminant town greeter was most anxious to show me something down in the barn... Feeling as I walked as I need to keep this at bay a little longer as my time here is non existent or limited it just is...

After showing me a old sign he was very amused by and to humor the mood I also thought it was a nostalgic . After most of the farm bid down sitting on the porch as most had kinda left me not in avoidance just end of day...

The mom came out with some coffee and we partook in a very interesting correspondence in a very peculiar matter, such as life, and similar and not so normal inquiry, and knowing my reason would be safe.

Next morning. After coffee of course most others had begun their day a not said welcome home...

Kinda nice but this isn't home, wish I could explain, but best to say it's like being set out in a big egg to a new world in toas new Mexico. They did pitch the idea to many civilizations but said it was far to supiror to be taken so realistic...

So for a time I watched this reason of being grow his mind ability far surpassed any we have ever known... But it was a great triumph,but yet debilitating defeat. As they won state his friend had a heart murmurs and it stopped... yet as I thought he was my purpose is totally oblivious to why? So the town did celebrate...

Oh yeah we won state and hope to next year... As my individual of interest who is always very informative. As I leave to find more reason why not so apprent I'm here.. it was before my eyes him and his buddy in a ghostly translucent attire. Talking sorta going through the motion of plays but one in particular.. huh I thought as I made my way,, seems our honestly friend fades, I said walking up..

Well he knows what you are but if not him then who? He asked with a certain need for urgency... with a sincere tone I assured him I did not know. So for a time life went on the boy and his friend enjoyed that year made playoffs, but that play he protected was the nail in the coffin.

So as that season moved on through the times baseball lost semi... Basketball was kinda a fill in boys gave there all but a team of 5'10 playing 6'2-6'6. Yes hight school it's kinda a no brainer but wasn't a terrible year just like I said feel in... Now back to football year 10. Hoping to repeat but better together... Well all seems up and ready to go first part of season, mid part well it's for ball, got in playoffs!!!

Was a rough fight but they did it going to the state… Well was a tough fought game not much first half expect a whole bunch of hair pulling and bruises. But they came back third quarter keeping it a one touchdown away. Until part way into the forth touchdown, with a two point.

Realizing the predicament, they went for it almost like a great come back with 7 seconds to decide on last time out.. they decided to qb sneak…

As he caught the ball tossed to the running back and then the running back throw to the qb just as he cleared the goal line, then taking a severe impact by three. Collapsed him.

With a few last possible movements as his body begin to go limp curled a fist and raised it. They did an on side kick recovered and decided on a frigid artic torment decided to kick… not made many not had to but actually better punter… but here he goes and how else could you end a Cinderella story… but by victory.

Well after time it was realized he would never walk in assisted by a chair, the impact was not for the faint of heart, as for the players they wish they had seen his number, he was just that kind of kid…

Well the fallowing year slow life for him, but now he is doing physical therapy and such... making great progress, and his buddy still here after all this time is far beyond even my logic and I do this for my reason.

Well time would pass sports fill in jamborees and of course football, and he has been co coaching being a student of many sports.

But this day wasn't as it should be, like I'm saddened by something, but why most interesting what, this is what I do collect the lost...

Periodically he seems to believe he can walk again been to long great strides but not in this life, but his buddy keeps believing...

Then that night he got in his chair rode it to the edge of the stairs stood straight up, causing the noise to awaken his mom in a froze delight watched him standing as he fell forward she leap from the bed as he stumbled down tne to the bottom, as she forcefully shoved his chair slamming it against the wall, by awakening his dad who came out to see as he sprinted down the stairs behind her. Only to have her stop him pointing as they watched their son stand up and walk out the door. As they rushed to the door the saw his friend helping the older lady in one car and their son was helping the girl in the other car. As they made safe distance for them the cars on collided and all dead on impact but two...

As their son returned to the house and reentered his body, I knew what I was sent to do...

As I touched his shoulder he begin to stand all mobility restored, and I for the first time floated, did see why I needed the ability to walk in a ghost...

And his friend well he's looking after things for me.

www.ingramcontent.com/pod-product-compliance
Lightning Source LLC
Chambersburg PA
CBHW031902170626
46807CB00004B/1857